Bear and the Dinosaur

By
Dyan Beyer

To order additional copies of this book, contact:
Xlibris
844-714-8691
www.Xlibris.com
Orders@Xlibris.com

ISBN: Softcover   978-1-6698-2863-1
        Hardcover   978-1-6698-2864-8
        EBook   978-1-6698-2862-4

Print information available on the last page

Rev. date: 04/03/2023

Written for my grandson, Bear Robert Beyer.

Grandchildren are a blessing and I have been truly blessed.
Each five of you have made my life so much better!

2 Corinthians: 5:17: For we live by faith, not by sight.

Other Children's books by Dyan Beyer

1. *Under Angels' Wings*

2. *Baby Boy Bear*

3. *Baby Grace Is Here!*

4. *Baby Needs Pants*

5. *Little Lion*

Once upon a time there was a boy named Bear. He loved dinosaurs so much he would go outside in his yard everyday with his dog, Mini, and try to find one!

Bear, with Mini's help, would dig big holes in the yard hoping to find a T-Rex or Triceratops. Those were Bear's favorite dinosaurs!

One afternoon, his shovel hit something in the dirt. Bear got down on his knees to get a better look at what he had hit. His little hands pushed through the dirt and he pulled out a small egg.

He didn't know what kind of egg it was but he was excited to find out.

Bear gently tapped on the egg not wanting to hurt whatever was inside. He gently shook it. He didn't hear anything. Mini came running over to see what Bear had found.

"What are you in there?" asked Bear.

Suddenly, the egg started to crack open. Bear held the egg with two hands, looking down in wonder as he saw a little green head appear.

6

"Wow, Mini, we found a DINOSAUR! But not just any dinosaur, it's a T-REX!" Bear shouted.

Bear was so excited, he could hardly believe what he and Mini had found.

"I found you in the dirt, T-Rex...or should I call you Rex for short?" Bear asked the dinosaur.

Mini sniffed at the newfound dinosaur while Bear wondered what he would do with Rex.

"Dinosaurs need food and water and someplace to live!" Bear said holding Rex in his hand.

I know, thought Bear, I will bring him to my Mom and she will help me.

8

Bear took Rex into the house. When Bear showed his mom the dinosaur he found, she let out a very loud, loud scream!

"AHHHH...BEAR...DON'T BRING THAT LIZARD INTO THE HOUSE!" yelled Bear's mom.

Bear never heard anyone scream as loud as his mother did when she saw Rex! Bear knew his mother did not like lizards but this wasn't a lizard...it was a T-Rex dinosaur.

"He's not a lizard, Mom. Rex is a dinosaur! Me and Mini found him in the backyard," Bear said.

Bear's mom laughed, telling him it wasn't a dinosaur but a lizard and would he please bring it back outside.

"But Mom, he is really a DINOSAUR and I need your help to take care of Rex."

Bear's mom told him she would help care for the little creature but Rex would live out in the garage!

Bear put Rex in the box with his mom's help. She told Bear to get some roots and grass to feed Rex.

"But, Mom, T-Rex dinosaurs don't eat plants or grass...they eat meat!" Bear informed his mom.

"Okay, Bear, I will bring out some chop-meat but put some grass in the box as well," said Mom.

Once Rex was settled into his new home, Bear got his dinosaur book and brought it out to the garage.

"Rex, it says that a T-Rex full grown will be 40 feet long and 12 feet high!" Bear said in awe.

Mini wagged her tail thinking Bear was talking to her, "Much bigger than you Mini!"

Bear patted Mini's head, "Mini, did you know that a T-Rex weighs about 11,000 pounds? And could grow, if well fed, up to 15,000 pounds!" Bear said, his eyes opened even wider now.

"Rex, how will I keep you in this box when you get that big?" Bear asked.

The next morning, Bear quickly got dressed and ran outside to see if his dinosaur was still in the box. Sure enough, Rex was snuggled up in the grass.

"Wake up, wake up, little dinosaur!" Bear said happy to see that Rex was still there.

The tiny dinosaur opened his eyes and he stretched out his short little arms.

"Morning, Rex, I was thinking I can take you for a bike ride today," Bear happily said.

Bear put on his safety helmet but didn't have one for Rex. "What can we use to protect your head?"

After looking around, Bear came up with the idea to cover Rex's head with a bandage.

"Do you want to ride in the basket or in my pocket?" Bear asked wrapping the dinosaur's head.

Rex decided he would rather ride in Bear's pocket!

14

"Here we go, Rex! Hold on, Mini!" Bear said as they went flying down the driveway.

"Isn't this fun, Rex?" Bear asked as he lifted his head up into the wind.

16

After the bike ride, Bear brought out some fresh water and more meat for Rex to eat. Bear wanted to play baseball but Rex was too small. He decided to bring him swimming instead. Rex loved the water and was a good swimmer. At the end of the day, both Bear and Rex were tired and went right to bed after dinner.

The next week Bear looked at Rex and he noticed that he had grown a lot! He no longer fit in the small box that his mother had given him.

"I need to get you a bigger box, Rex," said Bear.

He asked his dad to find him one so his dinosaur could live in it. His dad found him a box twice the size as the first one. Bear moved Rex into his new home.

20

"Today, Rex, we can go to the playground!" said Bear.

And off they went with Rex on Bear's shoulder.

They played on the slide and monkey-bars but Rex liked the swing the best!

22

Summer was over and Bear had to go back to school. He didn't want to leave Rex home alone so he decided to bring him along. He didn't think the teacher would mind, especially if he put Rex in his backpack now that he was too big to fit in a pocket. It wasn't until lunchtime that the teacher noticed a little dinosaur head sticking out of Bear's backpack.

"What is that, Bear?" asked the teacher.

"Oh, it's Rex, my dinosaur," answered Bear.

The teacher looked closer at Rex and said, "Bear, that is not a dinosaur. It's a lizard."

"No, he's a T-Rex dinosaur!" Bear replied very sure of himself.

He wasn't allowed to bring any pets, including dinosaurs, to school anymore said the teacher.

After school, Bear would go out into the garage and play with Rex. He was eating a lot and GROWING a lot! Mom gave Bear more meat and a bigger box! Bear's mom couldn't believe Rex was eating that much! She liked Rex as long as he stayed outside in the garage.

On Bear's birthday, he had a pool party. Rex was there and helped him blow out the candles. Bear's schoolmates really liked Rex and they thought he was very cool especially when he floated in the pool!

The months went by quickly and Bear and his dinosaur grew to be best friends. By Spring, Bear had to get an even BIGGER box because Rex had outgrown all the boxes! This time his dad had to go to the hardware store to get a crate large enough for Rex to fit in it.

"Son, it might be time to let Rex go. He needs more room to grow and live," said Bear's dad.

"NO, Dad, he's my friend...my dinosaur. I want to keep him!" Bear said with tears in his eyes.

"Bear, Rex is not a dinosaur. You can see that he's a lizard," Dad said.

"You and Mom always taught me that faith is believing in what you can't see. You said if I had faith as small as a mustard seed, I could do anything. You told me everyone sees things differently depending on God's Will. You can't see Rex as a dinosaur but I can. Did you and Mom lose faith?"

"No, Bear, just sometimes grownups need to be reminded about what we were taught and about what we forgot. Thank you for reminding us. You are right, we should live by faith not by sight."

"So I get to keep Rex?" Bear asked.

"It might be okay for now, Bear, but it's not fair for Rex not to be free. The Bible tells us that the heart of man plans his way but the Lord determines our steps. It may seem like our plan but it is always God's Plan. Our faith and belief in God allows us to do that," said Bear's dad.

Bear thought about what his dad had said about having faith in God's plan. He wondered if Rex really wanted to live in a crate or did God want him to be free out in the wild. He didn't want to think about it right now. He just wanted to keep Rex and be his friend.

30

By summer, Rex couldn't fit in any crate!

"Rex, do you like it here?" asked Bear not noticing his Dad and Mom had come into the garage.

"Yes, Bear, I'm sure he does but it's time for Rex to move on," said Bear's dad.

Bear held back his tears, trying to reach up to rub Rex's head and finding it difficult to do now that he was so tall.

"I want to do what is best for Rex, Dad. Where would he go?"

Bear's dad took a minute to answer, "I don't know...maybe where all the other dinosaurs are."

"Where are they?' asked Bear.

"I'm not sure but my faith tells me to trust in God. He will take care of Rex and put him where he wants him. You reminded me about having faith...do you remember, Bear, what faith is?"

"Yes, its trusting in God and believing in what you can't see...but won't Rex be afraid to be alone?"

"Rex won't be afraid and he won't be alone. God will be with Rex," said Bear's mom.

"How do you know that, Mom?" Bear asked.

"Because it was God who put Rex in that egg, it was God who allowed you to find him and it will be God who determines where he goes, Bear," said Bear's Mom.

"But how can you be sure...sure that God will take care of Rex?" Bear asked.

"Because it is His promise that He will be with you always. There is nothing to fear about being alone, Bear. God's promise is good and you can trust in His Word," said Bear's mom.

34

The next morning Bear went into the garage and he saw that Rex was not in the crate. Rex had moved on to be with the other dinosaurs. He felt sad and happy at the same time. He was sad that his dinosaur was gone but happy that Rex trusted in God and was free. Just as Bear was getting ready to go back inside, a little lizard crawled up on his shoe. Bear bent down and picked up the lizard.

"Hi there, little lizard. You're no dinosaur but you're close enough!"

Bear happily put the lizard, which he named Dino, in his pocket and went on a bike ride.

The End

Printed in the United States
by Baker & Taylor Publisher Services